Behind This Mirror

Behind This Mirror

stories

Lena Bertone

DURHAM, NORTH CAROLINA

Behind This Mirror

Published in the United States of America
Library of Congress Cataloging-in-Publication Data
Bertone, Lena
Behind This Mirror, stories / by Lena Bertone
p. cm.
ISBN-13: 978-1-949344-15-8

Author's Notes
Rebecca King and Sam Martone, thank you for your generosity and your enthusiasm, and for your all around awesomeness. Thank you to my dear friends and family, especially KP, SB, PM, DL, JS, and JP; and thank you with love to my sweethearts, W and A.

Cover by Savannah Bradley
Layout by Elizabeth Coletti

Published by
BULL CITY PRESS
1217 Odyssey Dr.
Durham, NC 27713
www.BullCityPress.com

Contents

Stories for Next Time

You might forget what you said yesterday. You might forget all of last year. You might forget to look for yourself in the mirror or what you're looking at in the mirror. It's not inconceivable that everything you have will be gone the next time you wake up or that you'll be able to hold it all in the palm of your hand: a globe you can see yourself in, all your stupid mistakes, all your glory.

There was a story my hand wanted to tell your hand, but your hand was gone when my hand went looking for it. Your hand did this thing: traced a picture on my leg, fingers intent on explaining something about a boat, a wind, I don't remember.

You were about to call me pretty, and then you left to meet your mother. I'm still waiting on this bed for you.

Do you know where you are, hand?

My hand has a story to tell you.

It's a miracle story.

Come back.

In the miracle story, a woman is sought out by an otherworldly presence. The spirit assures her that she is praying the right prayers to the right gods. There are rings and the names of real people involved, details that bewilder skeptics like us.

We're careful not to say nice things to each other. I don't like to say nice things to you because I don't want to jinx it. I poke you in the butt and say nice butt. I say your name. I put my hand in your hair. Once, you gave a short lecture on why my breasts are above average, even from the horizontal position.

Sometimes we do sweet things. I rub your back while we fall asleep. You hold my hand for a long time, stroke my knee in the middle of the night.

We're each shocked that the other does these things. We never say anything about it.

I wonder if you ask me that stupid question because you have nothing else to say to me or because you really want to know. You do it every time even though I've asked you not to. Do you want an alternate story? What I'll tell you: he's fine; I hate him; his health is constant, but he complains all the time; he's needy; if I get close I risk him touching me; him touching me is one of the things I hate most; this conversation is boring and useless and what good did it do us to have it again?

I knew a man once who frightened me with his caveman brow, his caveman intellectual I-will-crush-and-intimidate-you brow. It came with a caveman walk, long arms brushing the ground, a short hip bounce. When I got to know him, he swore he meant nothing by the brow—an unfortunate trait, that heavy ridge, that academic bone. He could do nothing about it. But what about his lips, then? I could have asked, but didn't. The big lips, the permanent pout. Everything about him pushed me away with enormous, hairy-knuckled hands.

Every time you leave, I realize that I've forgotten to ask you if you find me unattractive, or if you have sex with me because you pity me. Must remember for next time.

All day I waited for you. Tonight you call and tell me some junk about the moon. You tell me the moon is 240,000 miles away. I write it down so I won't forget. We see the same face, always, because it rotates and revolves at the same rate.

This is much less than I wanted, but I won't ask for more or complain that I won't see you. This matter between us is too delicate. It's a bauble, porous and bright, and I want to hold it, cheap thing, as long as I can before we crush it.

I've heard this story of yours before, in fact: many times. I don't mind hearing it again. You tell it the same way every time, as if the part you don't remember is me.

I think about your eyes when you're not here because I don't look into them when you are here. I mean I do, when we talk, but when we're not talking, it's too much. I do want to look sometimes. In bed, they're a lighter blue. I peek, but I have to look away. We are somehow, despite our unabashed activities, shy individuals. I don't want to assume such familiarity.

Once, I asked you over, and you said no, and in the conversation that followed, the static must have eaten your words, because I thought I heard you say something like: you're really good to me. I tried to reimagine the sentence. You're really into me? You're good at fooling me? You're really like food to me? I said: okay, you too. I think this means words don't mean the same things to us.

Next time I'll say: I didn't mean you when I said I have very low expectations. I'm sorry I said that. Actually I did mean you, but anyway I shouldn't have told you.

In the miracle story, the woman is healed of her disease. No one expects it. She doesn't die, year after year, decade after decade, and her frozen face stays lovely and smooth. One day, she breathes an impossibly deep breath from her fragile chest, and proceeds with her life as though she were the young girl she was before she got sick.

I knew a man once with sweaty palms. It's something you can forgive because you think: it's for the fear of me, and how nice that I inspire fear.

When you ask me again, I'll tell you that it wasn't so difficult to stop loving him, maybe because I hadn't loved him in a long time, maybe because I had said the words I love you without meaning them, maybe because the things I did for him meant the words I love you, but he didn't believe them anyway, so I stopped believing them too, and I stopped doing those things, and I stopped saying those words, and then it was broken, like a spell, it was broken, like a spell, it was broken.

I'll tell you how to make the cookies when you tell me you're not coming over anymore. I promise. Until then, I'll make them for you, and we'll pretend they're the reason you come over.

Every time I recommit to not becoming your girlfriend and you promise not to be my boyfriend, I think about the ways I could help you when you finally meet your perfect girl. You could kiss more gently. I could show you how to melt a girl like me. With the rest of your talents, such a skill would be deadly. I want to show you this kiss, but I keep waiting. These are not the kinds of things we say to each other.

Your name is Iran Ishemetz in my dream because my brain can't remember your once-mentioned, unpronounceable, Greek real name that's not your name anymore. Your mother took it away, and the only thing she gave you was clean laundry, furiously sorted, stacked into rectangular packets of order, crisp, smelling like water, blue like the Aegean, blue like a flag as if a flag means anything, blue like the eyes I find incongruent with the name you said that I can't repeat or recall.

Was this part a dream: when you asked me, what was your name again?

All day I thought about last night. I am so tired. I want to sleep, to not be doing anything that I'm doing. I try to concentrate on anything and I go back to last night. I think about how I can tell you how great it was, how great—a slippery term because it was intense, it was extraordinary, it was a thrumping, despite it not being, never being what I need.

Still: holy shit.

I wrote you a quick text after you left this morning, innocent-like, but I want to tell you that I've been thinking about last night all day. But we have restrictions. I don't want to call. I can't say it outright. I won't be needy.

Fraught is a bound-up word. All those letters, one utterance. Not taking any of those sounds to completion. Even that F. You start that F in the middle of that F. You don't even give that F its due.

It's a tangled word. It could rhyme with laughed or daft, but it doesn't. It could be as dusky or spare as drought, but it isn't. It could wear its sickness like cough or push you roughly, but it won't shout like that. Its weight clings to you like humidity; it's a croak you feel sticking in your chest that won't unhook itself.

I want to see you. Today the thought of him seized me again, the ghost of him, ramshackle bones clutching my chest. I was driving in my tin can car, the glittery blue swirling complications in the sun, shining all those stupid memories of him, radiating them through the box of my body, and this packed word fought and squirmed in its vessel, all that one sound meaning the thing that I was, untied inside myself.

Let's explain the things that happened. Let's say them again and again until we come to an understanding of all the things that went wrong. Maybe if we tell the stories again every day to each other in another new way or if we tell them again in just the same way, same words, same elocution, lip to lip, then the shape of the awfulness will appear like smoke in front of our faces, and we'll see what it looks like, see it for what it is, and blow it away.

It was hard to see it in the dark, as I sat with him on the porch swing and we drank beer and pushed with our feet, but we both had the feeling that the spark we'd first mistaken for romance was the tiny beginning of a black hole pulling everything—our beating hearts, our breath, the atmosphere—into itself, spiraling away in the night sky.

In the miracle story, the miracle hasn't happened yet. Will you be disappointed? I'll wait to tell you.

I knew a man once who held my hand because he liked to. Not because I wanted him to or because it was the next thing he was supposed to do. He knew what he wanted, and that was to hold hands, among other things that felt good to him. He was a manly man, which was confusing to me, because how do these things coincide? Manliness and wanting to hold hands.

I found our fingers joined in the middle of the night.

He needed to hold something tight.

He took my hand, my whole body, because it was there and wanted.

Inquiry

Do you practice to forget or does it just happen. Do street names disappear from signs, do signs blink and fade on the horizon. Shaped clouds fall off the sky. Barbers that remind you of uncles not remind you anymore. Does it take practice to forget a face. A sharp jaw or the name attached to that sharp jaw, imprinted in it and in your head when you see it move, when you see it shift into a smile at you. Do you remember how to smile, or when to smile, when your neighbor asks you about the old lawn mower in the shed that may or may not exist. How should you know, you wonder, when she asks you where you've been, all this time, in and out, away and back. Does it take practice to say the right thing or is it better not to try. Is it better to forget that she's there, with dirt on the knees of her jeans. Expecting an answer to her unanswerable question. You clear your mind—you have practice—and go see if it's there—this phantom lawn mower, which may have existed, which could have existed, for all you know—in the shed, preserved, filled and ready to run.

Better Days

On Tuesdays, she didn't sweep: she and her sisters ran barefoot through the house to see who had the dirtiest feet by nightfall.

The princess had a premonition that the queen would test her with a pea, so before she went to meet her prince, she stopped at the village inn and had a cinnamon spiced brandy with one of the king's horsemen, who loosened her corset as he twirled her across the floor.

Before the tower, and after the tower, her favorite game was tag because she was the fastest girl, and she could run from home until she was just a golden dot sweeping noiselessly toward the horizon.

The guy who made the magic mirror had a plane to catch and a beach lounger waiting for him in Santo Domingo, so he inserted a shoddy spell into the slot and didn't waste another thought on whatever hag would want a piece of painted glass reciting some nonsense about beauty.

Godmother overslept, and the girl missed the ball, but the next day she announced that she would pay her way through college instead, which honestly turned out to be much more fulfilling in the end.

The huntsman had no patience for the queen's bile or vanity, so he stole her stepdaughter for a day and took her go-karting, where he got the girl good and filthy, hair to toenail, exhausted and crusty, filled up on caffeinated orange soda and cheesy hot dogs.

Little man was spinning gold for damsels across five kingdoms, and as soon as he'd collected a big sack of jewels and trinkets, he sold them for a pile of cash and flew to Thailand for the operation he was sure would make him the person he was meant to be.

The king had doubts about the woman who would become his daughter's stepmother, but on their wedding day, she promised him a threesome with her erstwhile acrobat girlfriend, and that erased everything but joy from his furrowed face.

As the woodcutter sat on a fresh cut tree trunk and ate the cheese sandwich his wife had made for him, he saw a wolf pass by, and its swagger reminded him of a surly courtesan he'd had once at a brothel, which made his mind go to those bawdy, delicious places he knew it shouldn't go.

She could be a vicious bitch to her stepdaughter, but during a moment of conscience, she sent the girl out with her daughters and a hundred dollar bill so they could all get milkshakes and manicures while she stayed home and watched what was left of The Price Is Right marathon on the Game Show Network.

One night in the bath as she rubbed the glowing top of her belly with oil, she thought: instead of giving that dwarf my firstborn, I'll fake my kidnapping by bandits and leave all these bastards behind. Tomorrow.

He held the slipper in his hand and decided to take the day off from finding the love of his life—she would wait, and he would wait, and they would both do better having thought it over for another twenty-four hours.

Even on days when he didn't have a juicy meal, when all he managed or bothered to take down was a stringy old rabbit or a family of rats, the wolf licked his paws and remembered his best kills: the plump girls and boys he'd befriended first, who had slipped right in and allowed him to take the first bite.

Today, she didn't use the forest to get to grandmother's house: she just found a clear spot of grass and lay down, let the sun warm her face and dress.

Self-Portrait

Leo's wife Margaret noticed that the only self-portrait he'd given her was one of himself as a woman. Why? She wanted to know. Why that one? He assured her that it was the only one of himself as a woman so far. For her best friend, a banker, Leo had created a self-portrait called "Self-Portrait from Collage of Dollar Bills." The banker had returned it because it was a federal offense to defile paper currency. Leo's collection of self-portraits stacked almost one hundred deep against one wall in his studio, formerly their daughter Bettina's bedroom. In the two years during which he produced his "art," he had painted, drawn, pastelled, gessoed, charcoaled, color-penciled, and nontraditionally multi-mediated nothing but self-portraits.

"It is as though," Bettina, a college student at Binghamton, posited, "he is trying to find himself." Every weekend when she came home, Leo asked her to choose a portrait and discuss it with him over tea. Then he would commemorate the experience by sketching a portrait of himself drinking tea: pencil on napkin, pen on scrap of envelope, or smudge of jelly strategically blurred with drops of brown tea on café receipt. Leo collected these review-propelled self-portraits over many months to create a self-portrait from them titled, "Self-Portrait Created from Self-Portraits Generated During Critique of Self-Portraits." He used the information his daughter presented him about himself, his art, his self-art to inform subsequent self-portraits, and the work of his project grew more interior, retracted, self-absorbed, until he decided that his best portrait of self would necessitate Leo himself becoming the portrait. He retreated to his studio and shut himself in, out, and off while he meditated on how to make himself into himself.

"Your father is unbelievable," Margaret complained. "He won't come out of his room. Can you tell him, Bettina, that he is already himself?" The phone buzzed between them, Margaret's voice traveling through space to Bettina in Binghamton, Bettina's words reaching back invisibly to Margaret's ear, both of them confident they knew who they were speaking to and about.

Sorry

The instructions told me how to tell you to make that thing that you were supposed to make by that date that I thought you were supposed to make it by; I say I thought because I lost the instructions and told you what I thought they said about how you should make that thing, but when I found the instructions again today it turned out that I'd remembered them wrong, and the way that I'd told you to make that thing was not the way the instructions instructed you to make that thing so that the thing you made was not the thing you were supposed to have made according to the instructions that I read, or rather misread, then lost, then remembered, or misremembered, then found too late after you'd already made that thing you'd made by that date that you were supposed to make it by, that date being the one thing I did get right.

Lost Shoe

I lost one shoe in the basement, and now the basement's gone—swallowed into a swirling drain of mud headed California-wise through the earth. Funny thing is that the other shoe was there every time I checked, safe on a high shelf: lonely stack heel, stretched-out leather upper. It waited on that shelf, and I kept on checking, expecting the lost one to appear, return, un-vanish from nowhere but then the bottom fell out with a poof and the asbestos tiles turned to slippery dust, pulling in everything—and that other shoe fell in too, with the shelf it was on and the closet it was in and the poured concrete walls that surrounded it and crumbled, crumbled, crumbled into nothing.

Seven Sisters

Settesima's sisters tell her she has the hair of an angel, which is good, because looking at any other part of her is quite unpleasant. But her white blond curls fall to her shoulders, and they're so soft and shiny that the stranger can't help but sneak a touch as he passes her on his bicycle. He is riding past her, and he is so used to ugliness that it is easy to ignore her face, especially with the sun and the wind playing with the rings of her hair, as infatuated with them as he is.

Sesta's eyebrows take minimal grooming, and then they are like artwork on her otherwise hideous face. One might not even notice that they are too high on her endless forehead, because her brows are so dark and symmetrical, and move with such graceful emotion. Really: there is no reason to look at anything else on Sesta's face.

Quinta finds reasons to stick her nose in people's things. She desires connection. She wears large, dark glasses and a scarf on her hair and neck, lipstick and liner, foundation to hide as much as she can. But her nose: small, upturned, curious—a tiny person all its own—she wants to show you her exquisite nose, put it in your strawberries, your sleeve, bury it in your cheek to tickle and enchant you.

Quarta believes she can command with her chin. Once, on a crowded bus, she lifted it with medium force, and a man in a pinstriped suit stood and gave her his seat. Quarta's jaw is square but her chin comes to a pixie point. She has silenced crying babies with it. They look at her chin, entranced, eyes never wandering above that distinct triangle of courage.

Terza's sisters are jealous because she has two beauties: plump, heart-shaped lips so deeply pink they're almost purple; and when she parts them slightly, perfectly shaped white teeth with a translucent sheen. But Terza prefers not to smile due to the unfortunate circumstances of the rest of her face, which she tries daily to forget, except during Carnivale, when she wears a butterfly mask and flaunts her smile, her mouth as pretty as any movie star's.

Seconda's cheekbones draw attention as she walks, so she walks with her sisters to the Marketa, in the open air, where the sun's light catches the angles of her face. Heads turn and necks whip to see who belongs to the razor cheek strutting by. She's already past when they look, of course, so there is no seeing the rest of her face—unremarkable or worse—she does not allow it.

Prima's eyes inhabit her face with a largeness and ferocity that cause her other, monstrous features to pale and recede to an extent that, upon first look, might convince a young man to lock his eyes with hers, dark and sad, whites a shining white. Her lids dip down just sleepily enough to make Prima appear ready to close her eyes; indeed, when she blinks, her lashes link together for a long second before releasing, so that the young man watching might not be blamed for thinking that Prima looks upon him with wonder and disbelief, ardor and adoration, though when he tears his focus from her luscious, limpid eyes—that is, if he can—what he sees in Prima's face is something I would rather not describe here. It would be impolite. We all have flaws, every one of us. Prima, on the inside, is a lovely person.

Patch

Every night, she fought me on the eye patch.

"I can't see with it on."

"Just half an hour. Just one TV show."

It hooked over the left side of her glasses, but she'd lift it up to peek, or lift her chin to look under it.

"That's cheating," I said.

"I can't see out of my bad eye," she said.

Her bad eye: perfect, deepest brown encircling black.

We put a googly-eye sticker on the patch and looked in the mirror. She laughed, but she took the patch off. I made a deal with her: I would take off my own glasses if she would wear the patch. I'd offer my poor vision in exchange for her sacrifice.

She liked this game. She took my glasses and walked away.

"What can you see?" she asked from the kitchen.

"Not much," I said. "Shapes, colors. I know you because I know you, but not because I can see you, because I can't."

I let her hold my hand, and we went for a walk down the street, her with her patch, me without glasses. She kept asking what I saw, flowers and rocks and dried-up puddles. Can you see that, Mommy? Can you see this? As if I were seeing new things I'd never seen before. But I had seen all these things. Held most of them in my hand. A crumpled cigarette box; some random piece of litter that I could either pick up or kick away. She pointed them all out to me and I had to get very close to understand what each object was. Sometimes I would know from the smell before I was close enough to see or touch it. The best thing to touch, always, was my daughter's plump, bouncing hand. I lifted it to my lips and kissed the dimpled knuckles.

We walked past the Murphy house, one and a half streets over, and I saw something so big in their backyard that I could see it without my glasses. The arc of it hovered at the height of the roof, and I might have thought it was just a shadow from the house or the top of their massive willow tree, except that it hummed, or the air around it hummed, like a soft engine. I'd never seen it there before. I stepped closer, through their yard, leading my daughter in so that we could look back there and try to figure out what it was. My glasses were at home. I hadn't brought them, and I led my daughter back, into the blur of the Murphy backyard, where I'd never gone and never been invited. I felt lured in by the great dark humming shadow, and I couldn't tell what it was except that it was big and dark. I saw its outline, elliptical and unsteady like jelly, filled in blue-black and shiny, like a giant sea creature delivered on land. It was maybe a kiddie pool levitating on its side, or a trampoline lifted by the wind, or a half-deflated zeppelin, bruised and discarded. The unmowed grass tickled my ankles as I stared at the blurry black mass, trying to get it to focus before my eyes. Crickets whirred and I squeezed my daughter's hand as we took small steps toward the mysterious object. I heard a door creak and slam, and then one of the old Murphy sisters called from the deck: "Who is that? What are you two doing back there?"

As we got closer, the more it looked like nothing. A big, black clump of nothing; a charred black hole where a fire might have been: last night, last week, last time the atmosphere burned up. The sky glowed bluer around the dark shape, as if the proximity to darkness made the blue stand out in contrast. The darkness repelled the blue. And as the dark pushed the blue out, the dark pushed itself out too, and I felt it approaching me and my daughter.

It swirled and hummed and grew rounder, maybe trying to look friendly, or trying to look like it would take us in, but this seemed like a very bad idea. I couldn't see into it. Or there was nothing to see. I did not want to be embraced by this darkness.

My daughter, however, reached her soft, plump arm into it and wiggled it around.

"Can you see this, Mommy?" she asked. Her arm was in, and I couldn't see anything past her shoulder. The air around us felt thin and hard to breathe, as though the hole was sucking it all in. The humming stopped, or my heart was beating too loudly for me to hear anything else.

"Get your arm out of there, sweetheart," I said. My voice lay on the air where it had exited my lips, not moving.

I looked around for the old woman who had stepped outside, one of the sisters, but I couldn't see people without my glasses on. I could only see directly in front of my eyes. I reached out to pull my daughter away from the hole. It was easy: like it was nothing there in front of us, casting its shadow over us, enveloping her whole arm. I put her head to my chest, but before she let me lead her away, she stuck her feet to the ground, yanked the eye patch off, and chucked it into the middle of the darkness.

The Magician

THE MAGICIAN CALLS UPON

THE SPIRITS OF THE OTHER WORLD

TO ANSWER YOUR QUESTIONS

$2 FOR YES, $1 FOR NO

THE MAGICIAN PRESENTS

ORMANDO, THE LONELIEST MONKEY

IN THE TINIEST CAGE

HE LICKS HIS OWN TEARS

THE MAGICIAN REQUIRES

YOUR DEVOUT ATTENTION

AND UNGUARDED SENSE OF WONDER

LEAVE WALLETS AT THE DOOR

Are there any hungry boys in the audience? The Magician asked.

Many boys raised their hands.

I want the hungriest boys, The Magician said. Who among you are the hungriest?

Boys fought and pushed with thin arms until just three were onstage.

I haven't eaten in days, the first said.

I eat my own fingernails, the second said, and my sister's, too.

The third said, it's lucky that I have no food to eat, because my teeth are too soft and rotten to chew it.

You win, The Magician said. Now I wonder if anyone sees that bit of black bread on that high shelf?

The boys ran for the bread. The audience cheered. When they reached it, a trapdoor opened like a gaping mouth beneath them, and they all fell through.

The audience laughed and laughed.

Serves you right! The Magician said, for trying to steal my bread.

Behind this mirror, The Magician said, stands either a beautiful girl or my wife.

Laughter!

That's not funny, said a young woman with a hooked nose and a weak chin.

I like a girl with spirit and a great rack, The Magician said. He gave her his hand, and she stepped onstage. She tried to look behind the mirror.

That's not polite, dear, The Magician said, putting his hand on her waist.

She pushed it away. How am I supposed to see who's back there?

Let's have a chat first, The Magician said, taking her wrist and rubbing her rump.

She tried to wrench her arm free. Let go of me, she said, or I'll kick your mirror down.

She kicked it, and it cracked into many pieces.

You awful, ugly thing, The Magician said. You are very much like my wife.

He slapped her flat bottom.

Laughter!

In these lean, postwar times, The Magician said, we must sustain ourselves with whatever we have on hand. A volunteer?

A woman shoved her boy onstage. He tripped on the broken sole of his shoe. He's ungrateful, his mother said.

The Magician directed the boy to sit on a bench and showed him the swing of his pocket watch.

He turned to the audience. Hypnosis! he said.

Soon the boy was cutting the sole of his shoe with a fork and knife. He dressed the pieces with oil and vinegar, salt and pepper. Delicately, he savored every bite that entered his mouth, chewing each one almost endlessly.

Delicious, he said. The best roast beef I've ever had. Better even than my mother's.

A miracle, his mother said tearfully.

A line of people formed to the back of the theater.

THE MAGICIAN PRESENTS

POPO, THE OLDEST MAN ALIVE

WEARING THE OLDEST UNDERWEAR

APPROACH AT YOUR OWN RISK

THE MAGICIAN PRESENTS

THE AMAZING STORGA

THE HORSE THAT HAS NOT EATEN IN WEEKS

LIVE SHOWINGS TODAY ONLY

THE MAGICIAN PRESENTS

MAGIC BEANS BY THE DOZEN

RESULTS GUARANTEED

CASH ONLY, NO REFUNDS

He took off his top hat and displayed it, inside out, to the audience. He reached in with his arm, up to the elbow, pulled out a carrot, and tossed it backstage. He reached in again, up to the elbow, to the shoulder, and wrestled out a lean white rabbit by its ears and held it over his head.

Applause!

The rabbit squirmed and kicked its long feet.

What are you going to do with that rabbit? a husky woman asked.

I don't know yet, The Magician said. Are you making an offer?

I'll skin it and fry it, she said, if I can have half.

Let's make a deal, The Magician said. I'll take it all, but you can have the hat.

And what will I do with the hat? the woman shrieked.

Endless rabbits, The Magician explained. He dropped the rabbit back into the hat. It disappeared into the black.

No deal, the woman said.

Even the most dirty and destitute among you deserve love, The Magician said.

The audience was incredulous. They wanted to be convinced.

Take, for example, this man, The Magician said, and presented them with the smelliest, vilest creature possible, retrieved from a rescued garbage bag. His beard was wormy, his clothes fermented to his body. His rotten breath filled the theater. The clean poor swooned with disgust.

Even this man, The Magician said, has a contribution to make. This man is just like you.

Kill him! a child cried out.

The stench! a woman sobbed.

The Magician led the silent, crusty man to sit in a chair center stage. The grime on the man's face, like heavy makeup, absorbed the spotlight. The Magician pulled quarters from the man's ear and spun them into a bowl: tin for maximum sound effect. They spilled like water from The Magician's hand.

Applause!

As The Magician massaged quarters from the beggar's filthy ear, an old man gimped onstage.

What do you want, Old Man? Can you not see that I'm busy?

No, I can't, said the old man. He used his cane to feel his way toward the spotlight. He followed the sound of clinking coins.

Stay away from my money, Old Man.

He moved to the other ear, which released coins like a fountain. The old man, with his rigid gait, continued his approach.

The Magician slid out his fancy curled shoe and tripped the old man, who fell on his hip, his cane launching into the air, pennies spilling from his pocket.

I'm blind! he said. I want you to heal me.

The Magician caught the cane and twirled it. His white teeth glinted in the light.

Do I look like a healer to you? He picked up the pennies and threw them into the crowd.

THE MAGICIAN PRESENTS

BOOFO THE GIANT

HIDE YOUR CHILDREN

The Magician pulled an invisible string and released a noose from the rafters, climbed an invisible step stool and placed the rope around his neck.

Stop! yelled an old woman. What are you trying to do? You'll hurt yourself.

Just testing the rope, Mother, The Magician said. Would you like to test it in my stead?

The old woman waggled toward the stage, her thick hips shifting with difficulty.

Is that really your mother? murmurers in the crowd asked.

The Magician held both his hands out to the woman. She took them and stepped first onstage, then onto the unseeable platform beneath the noose. Her feet, beneath her long dress, were swollen around her slippers.

Who but a mother, The Magician asked, would be this stupid?

Mother, he said, the noose. The old woman slipped it around her neck.

And now I present—The Magician swirled his cape—appearing for the first time in public since her tragic accident: Lucintha, the dog-faced girl.

He swirled his cape again and again. Whorls of sawdust cycloned at his feet. The audience looked, mesmerized by the whoosh and clap. His feet danced in the dust. The light onstage dimmed. They all squinted to see the movement.

The blind man said, But where is the girl? His voice was absorbed in the group's shallow breathing.

The Magician swirled his cape.

I paid my ticket, the blind man said. Where is the girl?

Shut up, Old Man, The Magician said. I'm working.

I want to see the girl, he said. I want to see her with my hands.

The Magician swirled his cape furiously and then drew it up, revealing behind him, clutching at his backside, a tiny girl with the head of a dog: long snout, big brown eyes, pointy ears. A German shepherd.

The audience gasped.

Is it a mask? they asked. A trick? An illusion?

No, the Magician said. It was an accident. It was an accident of birth.

The tiny girl cowered behind the cape. When the Magician coaxed her snout, she snapped at him with long white teeth and grimaced. She hid her face with her girl hands and whimpered.

Leave the girl alone, they said. What have you done to her?

Small girls gathered in the pit. They reached out their hands to the tiny girl with the head of a dog. Come with us, they said.

The Magician pushed her off his cape. The tiny girl slid across the stage. See what you've done? he said. You've made them think poorly of me, Dog Girl. You've made them misunderstand, Dog Brain. Now: show us all a happy dance.

The boos and shouts quieted as the tiny girl stood and tapped out a gleeful dance, arms and fingertips outstretched as her heels and toes sang in speedy, sprightly snaps on the hollow wooden ground. There was no doubt, the way her fingers and wrists flicked to the music in her head, that she was a happy dog-child.

Fable

I looked in the mirror and saw a horse: the long face, the deep cavern below each dark eye, chin pulling down like a pendulum. You'll scare the child, I thought.

The house was dark day and night. I pulled the blinds shut every morning. For months, I slid around in socks and no shirt on. The baby awake for increments and then asleep again, attached to me like an animal and then tucked, ruffled, in her bassinet. I stood half-naked in the fridge, wept with yogurt smeared across my chest. At night when I opened the blinds, I exposed myself to the backyard. It sprawled out into forest and ravine. Glass-eyed, I focused on the line of turkeys by the neighbors' gate, gazed on two deer at the salt lick.

What are you looking at, deer?

When visitors came, I put on a stained shirt and let them in. Every one of them had a horse face! They'll scare the child, I thought. They looked at her, contorted, made animal sounds. I didn't know how she could bear it without screaming.

Missing

Some said a tiger returned from the dead and ate the missing babies, its eyes lit golden in the dingy brown of night. Others said they sprouted wings and flew away to America. Some thought they heard cries from a sealed cave, but it turned out to be hundreds of fruit bats, rabid and emaciated. The mayor was devastated by the news, even though the missing babies were just dirty peasants. Many potions for sadness were mixed and consumed; some were rubbed into the skin, and others burned like incense and inhaled. Upstairs neighbors had seen a suspicious couple with a wheelbarrow loitering in front of the building. Small dogs barked out pleas for the safe return of their tiny human companions. The mothers' bodies were exhausted with grief, but they couldn't recall where they had last left the babies. They'd put them down for just a moment, they swore, clawing through their hysterical tears: one moment of peace, of looking away, of imagining that they could be childless, and then it had become so.

Learning about Opposites

She asks me what the opposite of in the middle is. She's desperate. Her little voice quivers. I repeat it to my friends. We marvel and laugh at the cleverness, but she wants to know: what is the opposite of in the middle? If her vocabulary were more advanced, she would ask: what is the fucking opposite of in the middle? I don't know what to say. I think about a parallel universe invisible and adjacent to our own; the inside-out of a potato chip bag; turning a mirror around and looking into its back.

A crazy person gives my daughter a yellow ball he won at bingo. I use the word crazy all the time. It means everything and its opposite. It's very good and very bad, very emphatic and very bored. It's extreme no matter how I use it. The crazy person seems like a swell guy, with a soft, happy voice and appropriate questions like, how old is she? Has she started school? Isn't she a doll? They roll the ball around while another crazy person paces the ward with his iPod plugged into his head and his hands clenched into fists, catching my eye every time he passes the wired window.

All year I tried to forget the shitty things he'd done to me. It was excruciating at first, and then the rage and humiliation passed. After that, it wasn't even worth telling the story. Then, like magic, he forgot everything. Not just once, but every day, every hour.

What happened? he asked me. *What did I do?* And I told him. *I did that?* Yes, I said, you did. *I can't believe I did that.* Well, I said, you did. Believe it: you did. Then he would ask again, *What happened? I woke up this morning, but would you please tell me what happened?* A year of his life had been erased. He remembered me; he remembered himself; he remembered an imaginary life in which he had been happy.

Wolverine

Affectionately, he calls his girlfriend His Little Wolverine, and she is the least furry among us. Our hairlines are low, but not unnatural; our eyebrows joined but not unattractively so. Each of us has a mustache that she bleaches or waxes or shaves, or in Maria's case, wears proudly, faint brown hairs over the full curve of her mauve lips. We all have The Mole somewhere on our faces, from which grows the Lone Black Hair That Must Be Plucked. Stella's mole is below her left eye; Nadia's beside her right nostril. Vera and Lidia have theirs on opposite cheeks, and mine is at the classic forty-five degree angle above the lip.

Maria's boyfriend calls her Wolverine because when she tans to brown—in one afternoon, in her string bikini—that patch of hair on her lower back lights up golden against her olive skin. He offers to shave it for her, but she shaves her legs, and that, she says, is enough.

Our hair is brown—the kind of brown that people call black because it doesn't reflect—not red, not blond, not blue. Our eyes are like that too. The hair by our ears grows long, and as we grow older, more strays appear: chin hairs, neck hairs, chest hairs; freckles and moles pop and then hairs pop from them. Then the color of our hair fades, and the color of our eyes fades, and all that young hair, on our heads, our legs, our arms, it gets tired of growing. And eventually, we get old and everything fades to a clear gray, even our lips. And this boyfriend of Maria's, who called her Wolverine: he will be long gone.

The Magic Shirt

I wear the magic shirt when I want to feel sexy. I don't know what makes the magic shirt so special. It's black and sleeveless with untrimmed edging. It's a little low cut. I make sure not to wear a sexy bra with it because that would be too much. I only wear the magic shirt with jeans. It's getting old, the magic shirt, but people look at me when I wear it. They just look at me, or they say something like, "*you* look nice," when all I'm wearing is an old black shirt and jeans. The magic shirt is magic that way. It doesn't show much cleavage, but it shows the V of my chest, a hint of clavicle, and just the round edge of my shoulders. The magic shirt isn't tight, and it isn't loose. It requires no additional decoration. I lost the magic shirt once for a few weeks. It was a worrisome time. I've used the magic shirt for sexual purposes. I don't have much power in this world, but I have the magic shirt. I won't have it forever. One day I'll put on the magic shirt, and it will be ripped, or stained, or stretched out, or worse. The magic shirt will not be magic anymore. Then the magic shirt will be just a shirt, maybe even a shirt that won't merit wearing. What will I do with a shirt like that, that isn't magic anymore? What will I do without a magic shirt?

The last time I saw you was the last time I saw you. It was a long time ago, and the magic shirt was still bright black, no grizzle on the edge of the neck where you liked to touch it. When I last saw you, it was winter, and I wore two scarves, chest to chin, and a coat down to my knees. I paid for your nine-dollar cup of tea and mine with my credit card. We shared tiny shortbread arranged on the plate in the shape of flower petals, each cookie a teardrop, one bite. The shop was drafty, all windows, and almost as cold as it was outside. I kept all my clothes on. Underneath the humid frosty air that hung over us, that reached down from the high, punched-tin ceiling, we drank our hot tea and watched teenagers making out on the sofa three feet away. Under my puffy coat and scarves, under my pilly dotted cardigan, I wore my magic shirt, but you didn't see it. You put two fingers in the hole in the knee of my jeans. When I drove you home, you said that some day soon, you would get your rear window fixed and drive me around all day and night. I pulled my coat open when you kissed me and told you to kiss my neck, but there was too much scarf, and the air was too cold, and the magic shirt was hidden.

The next time I saw you, it wasn't you. It was a guy in line at the Hollywood with your hair, holding the hand of a girl who wasn't me. He turned around, and his teeth weren't your teeth, too white and too pointy. The shirt I was wearing wasn't the magic shirt, and when I got home, I tore through drawers looking for it. I didn't bother to turn on a light. I grabbed through balls of clothes, feeling for the undone edge, the fading ruffle down the front. I found it, crumpled and wan in a crowded corner. It had a mysterious stain on the belly. The fabric had worn so thin that in my hands it felt like nothing.

The Woman Who Waxed and Waned

They'd been sweethearts since childhood and had grown to the same height: five feet, two inches. They both had crooked noses and bright blue eyes. Of course they would get married, but they waited until they were twenty-four, when he would take over his father's iron-forging business. After they wed, her vivacious personality was taken over with depression when she found it difficult to become pregnant, and made worse when she had a miscarriage, and then the depression took over her body, and she was struck as though by a crushing physical illness. She lay in bed and wasted, losing what little plumpness she had, developing a troubling darkness under her eyes. The only thing that lifted her sadness was an unexpected pregnancy, and the couple had a girl, maybe the loveliest girl ever born, and they loved her as much as it was possible to love her. But the physical illness returned, a dark shadow under every bone, every bone evident underneath her skin, and the woman wore away until her condition was clearly terminal. The husband decided he couldn't care for her in that state, it was too much to bear, and he gave her back to her parents, his wife and their daughter, and lived on his own, expecting his wife to die. But his wife continued to live beyond her first death due date and then her second, and his daughter grew, and she grew to be breathtakingly, shockingly pretty. It hurt to look at her in the full light of day. She loved her mother and doted on her, caressed her withered fingers and frozen face. She loved her father, too, and would not tolerate an unkind word toward him. His wife continued to live, though she should have died. It was sad, all the years spent grieving, expecting her to die. She sat in a wheelchair, her limbs wasted, her speech slow, awaiting, like everyone else, her end moment. But instead of ending, years passed, and as they did, her gaunt cheeks began to fill again with flesh and fat, and sometimes, when she spoke, words came perfectly formed from her lips. Her breath always smelled faintly like flowers. She raised her arms and moved her fingers—slowly, it became clear that she was improving. Her daughter, now a teenager, took her for walks in the living room and later on the street. One day, the woman let go of her daughter's arm and walked a short length of sidewalk by herself, something she hadn't done in fifteen years. Soon after, she was able to style her own hair and laugh using all the muscles in her face. Despite the protests of her devoted parents, the woman took a taxi to her husband's house, wearing a new dress she had picked out and put on by herself. The next day, she called her daughter and told her to gather their things and come, so they could all be together again.

Exactly 69% of This Sad, True Story Is True

They'd been sweethearts since childhood and had grown to the same height: five feet, two inches. They both had crooked noses and bright blue eyes. Of course they would get married, but they waited until they were twenty-four, when he would take over his father's glassiron-forging business. After they wed, her vivacious personality was taken over with depression when she found it difficult to become pregnant, and made worse when she had a miscarriage, and then the depression took over her body, and she was struck as though by a crushing physical illness. She lay in bed and wasted, losing what little plumpness she had, developing a troubling darkness under her eyes. The only thing that lifted her sadness was an unexpected pregnancy, and the couple had a girl, maybe the loveliest girl ever born, and they loved her as much as it was possible to love her. But the physical illness returned, a dark shadow under every bone, every bone evident underneath her skin, and the woman wore away until her condition was clearly terminal. The husband decided he couldn't care for her in that state, it was too much to bear, and he gave her back to her parents, his wife and their daughter, and lived on his own, expecting his wife to die. But his wife continued to live beyond her first death due date and then her second, and his daughter grew, and she grew to be breathtakingly, shockingly pretty. It hurt to look at her in the full light of day. She loved her mother and doted on her, caressed her withered fingers and frozen face. She loved her father, too, and would not tolerate an unkind word toward him. His wife continued to live, though she should have died. It was sad, all the years spent grieving, expecting her to die. She sat in a wheelchair, her limbs wasted, her speech slow, awaiting, like everyone else, her end moment. But instead of ending, years passed, and as they did, her gaunt cheeks began to fill again with flesh and fat, and sometimes, when she spoke, words came perfectly formed from her lips. Her breath always smelled faintly like flowers. She raised her arms and moved her fingers—slowly, it became clear that she was improving. Her daughter, now a teenager, took her for walks in the living room and later on the street. One day, the woman let go of her daughter's arm and walked a short length of sidewalk by herself, something she hadn't done in fifteen years. Soon after, she was able to style her own hair and laugh using all the muscles in her face. Despite the protests of her devoted parents, the woman took a taxi to her husband's house, wearing a new dress she had picked out and put on by herself. The next day, she called her daughter and told her to gather their things and come, so they could all be together again.

Word Work

1: slower, shorter, slowest, shortest, sadder, biggest, bigger, saddest, faster, fastest

If you are slower, you are shorter. If you are slowest, you are shortest. Are you sadder than the biggest? Is your sad bigger than the saddest big? Who is faster than the fastest? Can the shortest be the saddest, or must you be faster to be sadder, the biggest sad running saddest and fastest?

2: book, moon, took, food, look, pool, zoo, noon, good, foot, instead, another

The moon book took too long to read. We used my good foot another way instead. You had that food look on your face when you told me about the pool at the zoo where they throw fish to the seals at noon.

3: brown, growl, now, down, how, clown, cow, crown, frown, town, eyes, never

The brown animal growled. Get down now, it said. It frowned like a mean clown. I looked at its eyes, gold as crowns. How had this brown clown animal entered town, growling. I heard a cow, then I was the cow. I had never been a cow.

4: mouth, house, found, our, out, cloud, ouch, shout, round, count, should, loved

Our mouth is as big as a house. He found our mouth and kicked us out of the house. The cloud said ouch in a shout that went around our mouth as big as a house. Around is not the same as round, but the sound is the same sound. A round sound coming out of my mouth. I should count the times he told me I had a big mouth. I should shout like a cloud with an open mouth. Ouch, I should shout, with my mouth big as a house. I found out that loved is not a round sound by our count.

Constants

Grizelda

We always called it The Appendage, even when Connie was little, and by calling it that, we pretended that it wasn't hers really and that it was useless. The doctors said it was caused by an engorged right ventricle and an unusually large subclavian artery entering her left arm. We didn't know this at her birth, of course. Her left arm was a little longer than her right, the hand a bit heftier and more animated.

She broke The Appendage when she was three, because it tried to pull out the yellow *Merge* sign at the edge of the front yard on the Park Street side. The wrist tore away, and the two bones of the forearm snapped. They took a bunch of X-rays then, and I remember they said her bones were unusual, or maybe that she had more bones than usual. I was seven then, and I don't remember much more than that.

When they set it in a cast, they said they didn't know how long it would take to heal. But Connie cried after the first week because the cast was tight. She said it hurt, and it looked like it was throbbing there at the shoulder, and then one morning when we woke up, the cast was cracked all the way down, and Connie looked sweaty and relieved. The crack kept getting wider until Connie laid down on the floor one afternoon and stretched out all over, and it popped right off. Preschool at St. Margaret's didn't work out for Connie because The Appendage wouldn't play nice, and kindergarten was harder because we couldn't pull her out. None of us really had an easy time with school because we were poor and that was bad enough, and we all had the same wiry orange hair. It was hardest for Connie, though. She was a smart kid, probably smarter than either me or Fiona. Connie was reading to us by the time she was four, and she could write her letters better than Fiona, despite being two years younger.

The problem was that while Connie was spelling words out in Mrs. Gibbon's first grade class with her right hand, The Appendage was crossing out her work with crayon, pounding on the table, jerking her out of her chair, et cetera. We were used to The Appendage at home, its tantrums, its stubborn streaks, like absolutely refusing to be clothed in anything other than the sleeve of my blue mermaid sweatshirt for an entire month of October. We could accept things like this. With school, it was different. Once, we tried putting it in a tight sling against her chest, but she came home with fabric burns on her neck and big finger mark bruises on her side.

Eventually, it learned to write letters and numbers and slapped at Connie's right hand for the privilege of doing math worksheets. Its handwriting wasn't bad, and Connie got the award for multiplication tables in the fourth grade. Looking back, those were the most peaceful years of our childhood.

The Appendage went through puberty before Connie, and it grew muscled and hairy, and its knuckles got tall and pointy, and its fingernails were thick and had long white moons. We were all a little afraid it, but Connie was protective. It had its moods, but it was part of her. It punched her once in the eye when she was shaving it, but it was remorseful afterwards, and as far as I know, that hasn't happened again. In school it was a problem because it used profanity, and it was belligerent with authority. Connie got suspended twice her junior year because of fights; stupid kids who didn't know better than to say things about The Appendage. She cried. She cried a lot. We all did.

The weather here does that to you. Even in the summer, the sky is like a dome made out of gray bricks, pressing down. And that's the happy time of year. Winter, it's hard getting up in the morning. It's so dark and cold, that cold air whistling through the window, the ridge of ice on the inside of the glass. Breathe on it and it goes white, like it's remembering how cold it is. One thing I can say about The Appendage is that it pulls its weight around here. It does a great job with the snow. Connie's the only one of us with waterproof boots, and that's all we need. I hate the snow, and I'm happy to let The Appendage clear the way so that I can wear my sneakers to the car. It does such a good job that I'll just wear my slippers if all I have to do is go out to McDonald's or Eckerd's and come straight back.

Connie's got one of those face masks that you pull the string, and all you can see are her squinty eyes, crying from the cold. They go out there together, and The Appendage takes a shovel to it, metal-edged with the comfort handle. They're out there, at it: scrape as the shovel drags across the gravel, clap as the snow falls aside, scrape, clap, at five-thirty in the morning because Connie's on first shift until the end of March. I'm hoping by then that it'll warm up and stop snowing nearly every day.

When Connie graduated from high school, Fiona and I were set up in our jobs and trying to take classes at the community college. It's always been hard, getting enough money just to live, but at least we have the house and each other. We never did much with the classes; it seemed stupid to waste all that time when we could be working and living. Then The Appendage landed a job at Chrysler, and it's really the one that takes care of us now, and Connie, of course, but it's hard giving up old ways, and Fiona and I still work even though I guess we wouldn't have to. We could take classes now, or get married, but it wouldn't seem right to take advantage of The Appendage like that. We never admitted to liking it, we were never its friend, we never had much more than disgust and fear and revulsion toward it when we were growing up. Now it's the man around the house, and I would miss it if it were gone. It's like having someone looking after you, or like the ghost of someone looking after you.

Fiona

Every time we visit Mom at Loretto, the receptionist says to me, A name like Fiona—that's like trouble walking in the door. She never says a word to my sisters, but then I'm often the one to speak for the three of us. It's off-putting, but that's the way it's always been. I'm the pretty one. People like to look at me, and I tell them what we're here for.

With Mom, it's the same as always. She's been in here forever. Old, infirm, incontinent, and whatever else, and the nurse is different every time. They say turnover is high in the health care profession. I know I wouldn't want to do it.

It's just something we do, this visit. She doesn't remember us. It's been about a million years since she was really around. So we sit on the bed, and Zelda combs what's left of her hair, and I rearrange the doilies on her bedside table, and Connie reads to us from the newspaper so we won't have to sit there in complete silence.

It's because of Connie that Mom's here, otherwise we'd be taking care of her at home, which, excuse my bluntness, would be a bigger pain in the ass than I could stand, considering everything else I have to go through for this family. But Connie makes a really nice wage from Chrysler, and that pays for this, and for her own therapy. Physical therapy. It isn't the arm that needs it; it's the rest of her. It's got to be hard, that thing pulling her around all the time, and then working on a line with robots the size of Oprah's walk-in closets. It's not so bad now in the winter, but in August, it gets to be 120° in there, or so she says, with the fire and the bits of hot metal from the smoothers, and the bodies of all those men sweating and panting, waiting for the buzzer.

But I don't feel sorry for Connie. She should consider herself lucky to have what she has, and Zelda too. Things could be a lot worse for them.

I worked at Learbury's until it closed a few years ago, and that place was a sweatshop in the summer. I didn't work at the steam presses, but close to them, at the sergers, and it took until last year for the calluses to completely smooth out, even with cocoa butter and vaseline used in combination. I work at the mall now. It's better for me. My face was going to waste working in a factory. The pay's not as good at Kaufmann's, but we don't really need the money, and I get a discount on everything in the store, including cosmetics. I'm going to take a class in medical transcription this summer. They say it doesn't take long to get certified, and then I'll have options.

Zelda works at Bristol Myers Squibb. I guess we're all lucky to have jobs. Zelda's and Connie's are good, long-term jobs. They're putting away money for retirement. Zelda doesn't like to talk about her job. It has to do with animals, but she never talks about them, which I think I would because I love animals. They probably like her there because she's been doing the same thing for a lot of years, and she's quiet. She doesn't complain much, at home either. She always has that wrinkled pug look on her face though, and some days her back is hunched more than others. I think she's getting a hump, but I don't tell her because what would be the use. It's not like having a hump detracts from her attractiveness, because frankly, she doesn't have any. Her legs are skinny and crooked, pointing out at the knees, and her head's bumpy, which she makes worse by cutting her own hair and cutting it so close that it looks like a bristly dented peach. And she's been wearing the same winter coat since holographic mittens were in fashion for eight-year-olds, which, that might be coming back, but still. There wouldn't be much hope for her even if she did clean up a bit. She's empty. There's no radiance there, like I have. And I say that not to be mean, but with all seriousness and in the interest of truth.

Truth.

This thing about options is bullshit, and I know it. Lucky, lucky, bullshit lucky. What is lucky about my life? I should be in some other fairy tale. I am the beautiful and long-suffering sister, but I suppose it's unreasonable for me to think that someone is just going to come into my life and sweep me away from this place, this place that's an iced-over cave six months out of the year. But I dream. I'm still beautiful. I'm the only one of us that got strawberry blond hair, and I smooth it out into waves. I have freckles. I can sit outside on the lawn chair in the summer in my bikini, and guys will slow down for a minute while they're driving down the road. We go to the farmer's market on Saturdays when it starts in April, and I can get free stuff when I'm walking by myself. I pick up a tomato and admire it, and I get a bag of them for next to nothing. When I'm with my sisters, everyone looks away.

It's walking distance, and on Sundays, I used to go by myself. It's a flea market on Sundays, and I think I was hoping to find something magic, maybe a ceramic frog I could kiss. A book of spells. A mummified prince. But I don't know if I'll go this year. It's too hard dreaming. When I was little, I had the sense that I was good, and that I would be rewarded. But it's hard when you're poor. You don't necessarily have a fairy godmother who's going to bring you a prom dress, and your sisters being weird really brings you down in the eyes of your peers, even handsome young men who are supposed to overlook that kind of thing.

We've been living here together, just the three of us, since we got Mom out to Loretto, and it just feels wrong and wronger every day, every week, month, year. I should be married. I should be far from this ugliness and cold. I should be summoning some power to make things different, to get me back in the game. I should be having beautiful babies. But I wake up every morning, and the sky is like a ceiling, and the driveway's clear, and I do the same thing I did yesterday and the day before for about a zillion years going.

But spring comes and it changes things. Maybe I'll feel different then.

Connie

We live in a shabby little bungalow at the end of Old Liverpool Road, where the 81 overpass sends cars over the rail when the temperature goes down below zero. Not just one below or two below; it has to be at least twenty-two below, and the most common air temperature not including wind-chill that results in a flying automobile is twenty-eight degrees below zero, when it's been that temperature or thereabouts for up to a day after a heavy snowfall. They say it's because the salt doesn't melt the ice when it's that cold.

I want to renovate our house someday. It's a bungalow with all the classic features. It's got the Arts and Crafts details, carved molding that goes on for days, like it's telling a story to the walls as it winds around doorways, up the staircase wall, along the upstairs hall. We've had this house since before any of us were born. It's the one thing we've actually owned all these years, and we're the only ones left here on this bit of crumbly road. The overpass is almost directly over the roof about thirty feet up; the road to Carousel Mall is across Park Street from us; there's a stadium named after a grocery store behind us, and the farmer's market and the hot dog house are walking distance, but we hate walking. There's a sewage treatment plant on the city side of the mall, and in the other direction, the village of Liverpool, which used to be here, is down Old Liverpool Road a couple miles now by the lake. The lake used to be a resort area—there were hotels all around. It was a destination. But there was also a chemical plant, and they dumped sludge into the lake until it died. Probably back then you could see the lake from our house, or maybe if our house wasn't built yet, definitely from the Victorians that used to stand next to it on either side.

Those came down in the seventies, I think, and somehow our little cottage got left behind. Sometimes I think they'll be knocking on the door to tell us they'll be tearing it down tomorrow. But it hasn't happened yet.

This has been a bad year for the cars. The first one went over the guardrail on December twenty-ninth and landed grill first on the double yellow line and then flipped onto its top. The lady in it was killed. I was at work. Luckily, though it was a post-holiday shopping day, it happened at eight a.m., so the traffic was still light. I watched out my window all day on Sunday, because that's what happens, when the weather conditions are like this, another one can happen. And I saw an SUV sail over the rail like it was a ski ramp. It flipped and spun, a tight twist around itself before it landed half on the road, half in our front yard. This was at ten at night, lucky again, because there's no reason for anyone to be driving down our road at ten at night, and the only ones killed were the man and his wife, who were coming home after a day of skiing at Greek Peak and dinner at the Community Restaurant in Cortland. All this information from the newspaper, of course.

There will be another one, because these things happen in threes. I try not to wait for it. I try to just go to work and do my best and shovel all the snow with my strong arm, and I try to be good to my sisters, who are my companions.

We've had 125 inches of snow so far this year. The accidents happen during the bad winters, and those come one about every ten years. Every few decades, there's an extra, stray bad winter that's worse than the rest, and I'm hoping that's not this year. I've already lived through one, and I don't want to live through another.

I was very small the last time, too young really to remember, but I remember it in my body, how the cold felt sharp on my eyeballs, and how my nose hurt, and then froze so that I couldn't feel it anymore. I remember the place between the top of my arm and my shoulder, where the jacket was cut and a bigger sleeve sewn on—I remember how I could feel the cold like ice cubes on my skin through the stitches. We were standing in the yard. I don't know what we were doing. I heard a noise that sounded like a moan from the sky, and I looked up, and there was a truck flying, but it was funny, because even more than the truck, I could see the sky coming forward like a big warm blanket, dark and woolly over us. The truck boomed when it hit, and it sent snow and glass through the air like a splash of water. Glass shot straight from the windows of the cars it crushed, and I was on the ground without having realized it, my arm cranked over me and pinning me down into the hard snow. Zelda got the worst of the debris. I think something thunked her on the head, maybe a door handle, because there was blood and Fiona screaming and crying as she ran inside.

That was the first of three that year, but the only one I saw happen. I ripped my jacket that day, and we didn't want to go into the yard after that anyway because of the glass. We don't play in the snow anymore, so that's not a concern. We just don't want people killed in the front yard. But there's always the matter of attention, of drawing attention and how that feels. The newspapers come, and so far this year it's been John Stanley from the *Post Standard* who knocks on our door and tries to ask us questions. What's it like living under the most dangerous overpass in Central New York? How many times has this happened in your lifetime that you remember? Cold's been a bitch this year, eh? Fucking arctic winds.

They think they can say fucking to me after they find out I work at Chrysler.

When Channel 3 came last week, I got Fiona to go out there for us. She's photogenic. People like to look at her, which is nice because then they don't look at me.

It's a curse and blessing living in this house, like everything else. If the wind is coming from the south, the overpass blocks most of the snow from landing in our yard. Taking a left turn out of the driveway is exhausting when the traffic is heavy, because you have to look left and right and up, and squeeze in where there really isn't room, and hope the antilock brakes work for when you speed up and slow down really fast at the light.

They're finally talking about doing something about the overpass. Nothing drastic, just a new policy that the guardrails have to be scraped off so the snow doesn't build up. It's funny that I have mixed feelings about it, because I don't want anyone to die like that; I don't want anyone to die at all. I guess it's just that I have a picture in the back of my mind that I like, that someday a car's going to come flying off the highway and land on the house. Maybe an eighteen-wheeler, and the house will go poof, and we'll all disappear.

Picnic

Her mother had been predicting her demise since childhood, so it was like a thunderous relief when she saw the strike from heaven, the white embrace of light, the electric charge that tied her down and lifted her up in the same glorious moment. And in that last moment, that blast of light and noise that, as far as she could ever know, would annihilate everything—the thing that was great about that split second was how perfectly it made everyone around her look and sound like a fabulous tableau in a '70s Broadway musical, like *Hair*, or *Jesus Christ Superstar*.

The Sleeping Woman

At first, I took catnaps on the sofa. Ten minutes. I just needed to shut my eyes. Then I slept sitting up while eating dinner, food in my mouth or a drink dripping out of one corner. I was so sleepy—so I slept all night, having long dreams about another life I lived on a silent beach, juggling baskets, and in the morning, I drove to work and fell asleep on the way, watching the road and traffic lights through my eyelids and waking up just in time to not collide with the cars or small animals interfering with my remarkably straight path.

But one day, I lay down in the morning, and when I woke up, it was night. I felt something in my belly—a cringe, a flinch, and when I looked down, I saw a bump there—a swollenness that had grown in just the time it had taken me to catch my breath from this awful aching sleepiness. It looked like a jelly roll under my shirt.

"Smith," I said. "Come look at this."

My boyfriend came out of the bedroom and looked down at the odd thing. I lifted my shirt, but it was under the skin, this log of something, this fleshy lump.

"How long was I asleep?" I asked him.

"I don't know," he said. "Just since this morning. Maybe yesterday." From then, I could not stay awake. And when I did wake up, my belly was larger. I fell asleep at work and woke up at home. I fell asleep grocery shopping and woke up in the car. I fell asleep on the bathroom floor and woke up at a birthday party at my grandmother's house.

"You must be hungry," she said as I staggered out of her den, a protrusion I didn't recognize extending from large pants that I also didn't recognize.

Yes, I was hungry. But I fell asleep, and when I woke up, I had partly chewed rare steak in my mouth.

"Where are we?" I asked my boyfriend, who had finished his steak and was waiting for me, who looked like he had been waiting for me for a very long time in a restaurant that was dark and empty.

At home, my favorite place was the Persian rug left by the former owners. It was red and brown with a big soft pad beneath it, and it swirled with lush flowers that I could lie against and trace with my fingers and stick my nose into and inhale. When I fell asleep on it, I could sleep for days.

The next time I woke up, I was in a hospital bed. My belly was covered with a sheet. I looked under the sheet, thinking there must be something there other than me, but no: all me. My skin was stretched and powdery, mountain-like. And there was movement on the mountain. An imminent eruption. Indigestion, perhaps. A doctor came in the door, wheeling a nursery cart.

"Congratulations," she whispered, and she smiled a very white smile. The baby was swaddled completely and turned to its side. I could not see its face. "Wait," I said, pointing at the mountain. "What's left in here?"

I slept again and woke up in a barn on a bed of straw. "Smith," I said, "are you here?" I shouted, but it came out a whisper. It was dark, but I could smell the dank water, the animals.

"Congratulations," he said. "They're beautiful." His teeth and eyes were shining and bright, and he was cradling a pair of pink and brown piglets.

I looked at them: they were perfect, downy and still moist. "But Smith, I think there's more." My body rumbled. A leg, then a hoof circumscribed an arc across the globe of my belly. I've always loved goats! Dear God, I thought: let there be goats.

But there were no goats. Instead, a donkey, and it was long-legged and loud, braying and kicking. I screamed, but it screamed harder, the tangle of legs pushing and burning its way up my body as its head ripped its way down. I would die, I thought, or pass out. I passed out.

When I woke up again, Smith was crying, and there was a bare bougainvillea bush lying between us. "Where are the flowers?" I asked. They were my favorites: the paper flowers, like tiny lanterns, so fragrant and delicate.

His head was down, and he held one green branch between two fingers. "They didn't survive." He could barely say it.

I wanted to console him, I wanted to cry with him, but I was so tired. "Smith," I whispered, but only because it was easy. Only because his name sounded so much like a breath.

The Magician

He sawed her down the middle and lifted a section out. It was no trick: he gave the bloody piece, spleen, appendix, gallbladder, to a little girl to take home as a souvenir. He was careful not to remove anything vital, but she was two inches shorter when he pushed the pieces of her back together— firmly—and asked her to stand and spread her arms and show the audience her smile.

The next show, he couldn't avoid a piece of her stomach. A few yards of intestines. The crowd screamed, men and women both. Little boys cried.

Her appetite suffered. Her costume drooped. Feathers and sequins that had once stood taut against her skin sagged and bounced.

Can't you work some other part of my body? she asked.

The next night, he cut off her feet. She wore her peacock blue slippers, and he gave one bloody foot to each of two pretty young girls sitting in the front row.

What kind of awful trick is this? the dark one asked. Her friend dropped the foot and ran.

What kind of trick? The Magician asked. Look, he said. Look: the girl survives.

The Bed

For the last 458 days of my life, I have made my bed. Tomorrow morning when I wake up, I will make my bed. If you were a stranger walking into my apartment, you could look down the short hall and through my open bedroom door to see that my bed is made in the style my mother taught me, the blanket smoothed across the width of the bed and tucked up under the pillows, then drawn over them to the headboard. This bedmaking might not seem unusual except that I had never before, in my adult life, made my bed. Do other people make their beds? Maybe this is normal. Maybe it's normal that I should decide unfailingly to make my bed, identically and perfectly every morning, the blanket falling from each edge in equal measure, a neat cone pleat at both bottom corners. A recurring visitor asks, do you make the bed because I'm coming over? I say, no, dear. I make the bed because I make the bed.

I make the bed before I leave in the morning. If I don't make the bed, I don't leave. Will I be late to work? I still make the bed. Will I have time to eat if I make the bed? Of course: I can chew while I make the bed. Sometimes I dawdle and run out of time to shower, but there's always a minute to make the bed. I may rush to get my child on the bus because I made the bed but forgot to pack her sneakers. I forget a lot of things, but I don't forget to make the bed.

One time I forgot to make the bed and I came back and made the bed.

One time my child threw up blood and I took her to the hospital instead of making the bed.

One time I slept on the sofa so I wouldn't have to make the bed.

I make the bed the way my mother taught me, the way she's made the bed since she was a child in Italy in a house full of children making their beds. It's the most Italian thing I do, making the bed. I have noticed this mania among Italians, that they must make their beds upon waking, that their bedspreads must be even and flat, that the pillows must be orderly, tucked simply and plumply, without ornament, without clamor, without fuss or frou. They don't make the bed to show off. They make the bed to make the bed.

Before the last 458 days of my life, I slept on a bed in my parents' house and I never made that bed. Before that, I slept on beds in houses I owned with a husband. I don't have that husband, those houses, those beds anymore, and I never made those beds. I didn't crave the order of making the bed. I didn't see the beauty. My mother's girlhood bedroom was little more than a closet with a window that opened to a garden terrace. Every morning until she was a woman ready to marry, she buried and tucked every wrinkle and fold of well-worn linens, snug like skin, around a narrow mattress. Now I'm nearly twice her age then, with a bed twice the size of hers, and it's all my own. I dress it with cotton sheets and a serious quilt: one somber color and a close pattern of stitches puckering the layer into an object that lies heavy over my body at night.

When I pull back the quilt and lie under the sheet folded tight against the mattress, my feet flatten and my eyes close, and my breathing shallows, and I think of nothing.

I think of sadness. In my bed, I imagine unfurrowing the muscles of my face, those places around my eyes and lips that pinch and make me think of the old woman I will someday become. I look into the darkness of my eyelids. I think of the man who doesn't want me, the one I still love, and the one who made me miserable for so long. I think of how that was my own fault. I think of how far I am from my past and my future. I think of the dread I feel every day, and most minutes of most days. And I lie in this bed. How good this bed feels. How good it feels when my visitor is here to share it with me, and how good it feels when I'm in it alone, like now, with my feet flattened and my breath low and me so slight under these covers that in the dark early morning, when I slip from my bed, I'll just have to gently pull the bedclothes back into alignment, my geometric quilt so orderly in its swoop over the pillow, neat and consistent under my fingers.

My mother says that making a bed is a two-person job. I always helped her make the bed: stood on the opposite side and pulled up the blanket as I paralleled her motions, both of us ending with the final one-handed tuck under the pillow. Now I go from side to side, making and adjusting to get the same effect. I spent so much of my life not making the bed, but making the bed was there, in my hands, waiting for me. I followed my mother in many ways, some of which I regret, but one I'm grateful for is the made bed. It means almost nothing, but I do it every day. I'm afraid of not doing it. I'm afraid of the day that I don't do it.

What will happen that day? Let me tell you: many things have fallen apart, but my bed is one thing I have made over and over again. Every day when I'm finished, I think: that bed is made for today.

Acknowledgments

The author would like to thank the journals where these stories originally appeared:

100wordstory.org	"Picnic"
apt	"The Magic Shirt"
Atticus Review	"Patch"
Caketrain	"Stories for Next Time"
Corium	"Inquiry"
decomP	"Missing"
Gigantic Bodies	"Fable"
Harpur Palate	"The Magician"
Matchbook	"The Sleeping Woman"
Monkeybicycle	"Better Days"
NANO Fiction	"The Magician"
theNewerYork	"Sorry"
PANK	"Self-Portrait"
Paper Darts	"Wolverine"
	"Exactly 69% of This Sad, True Story Is True"
Passages North	"The Bed"
Redivider	"Constants"
Salt Hill	"Word Work"
Syracuse Connective Corridor Exhibit	"Lost Shoe"
Wigleaf	"Learning about Opposites"
	"Seven Sisters"

About the Author

Lena Bertone is a writer and teacher in Central New York. She's the author of *Letters to the Devil* (Lit Pub, 2015). Her stories have appeared in *Salt Hill*, *Wigleaf*, *Passages North*, *Sundog Lit*, *Caketrain*, and other magazines.

About the Reissue

Behind This Mirror was originally published by Origami Zoo Press. The Bull City Press edition adds new stories, "Word Work" and "The Bed," as well as a new design.

This book was published with assistance from the Spring 2020 Editing and Publishing class at the University of North Carolina at Chapel Hill. Contributing editors and designers were Natalia Bartkowiak, Ashlyn Beach, Savannah Bradley, Elizabeth Coletti, Abby Davis, Deborah Gardner, Clayton M. Hall, Victoria Orbison, Kelsie Roper, Julie Salemi, and Adair Tompkins.